# Dedicated To

My parents who believed in me

My children who inspired me

Snowy loved the sun on her back as she ran around the backyard. What a beautiful day, she thought. As she looked up, Zoey, her best friend in the whole world, fluttered by. Snowy loved to play with Zoey!

"What should we do today, Snowy?"

"I heard there is a new virus, Corona that has changed the world. I would like to see how."

Snowy and Zoey made their way to the river, hoping their friend, Chloe, the duck was there. Maybe she knows how the world has changed.

On the way, they spotted a black cat lying on the grass. Snowy asked her, "Do you know how the world has changed?"

The cat lifted her head lazily, "the family I live with never leaves the house, and they want to stroke me all the time, and I hate it, that is how the world has changed," and she closed her eyes and went back to sleep.

At the river, they spotted Chloe swimming and splashing away. "Look at me, Snowy and Zoey, I am in crystal clear water, it is so clean and pure, there is no garbage or oil, and I think that is how the world has changed."

Suddenly the air filled with a loud noise, the friends looked up to see their friend Joey above. "Snowy, Zoey, and Chloe, you must come with me right away; I have never flown in skies that have no pollution or smog. I think that is how the world has changed".

As they reached the forest, Zoey stopped and took a deep breath. She had never smelled the flowers so fresh.

Joey flew up and up in the air watching all the forest animals below grazing on thick shrubs. Chloe waddled around, feeling the rich soil beneath her webbed feet.

A brown moose strolled by, and Snowy asked her if she knew how the world has changed.

The moose told Snowy how the forest has become full of clean things to eat, and that is how the world has changed.

Her friend, the squirrel, told Snowy how rich his pile of nuts has become.

The woodpecker told the friends how beautiful the trees have become, and that is how the world has changed.

Snowy, Zoey, Chloe, and Joey walked through the forest and into town. They could not believe their eyes!

No people anywhere! Where is everyone?

Shops closed. Garbage cans empty. No cars and no buses on the street. No noise at all!

The friends all said, "That is how the world has changed."

In the town, they met some of their neighbors, John the Rabbit, Mary the peacock, and Andy the turtle.

Zoey asked them if they knew how the Corona has changed the world.

John told them how he loves the empty streets, and he can finally wander freely anywhere he liked, and that is how the world has changed.

The friends enjoyed their adventure into a beautiful new world, full of clean rivers, clear skies, fresh forests, and empty towns.

As they made their way back home, tired but oh so happy, they wondered if the Corona came to remind us all to keep our earth clean for all creatures.

The End.